All proceeds go toward NY Unlocking Futures programming.

Trust Takes A Chance

By Ade & Claudette Faison

Edited by Nubia

Artwork by Edgar Plummer

Trust Takes A Chance

ISBN: 979-8-9985793-3-2

Library of Congress Control Number (LCCN): (Pending)

Published by: Claudette C'Faison

Published in association with NY Unlocking Futures www.nyunlockingfutures.org

Printed in the United States by: IngramSpark www.ingramspark.com

Illustrations by: Edgar Plummer
Contributing Editors: Tiffany Lachhonna, Na'ilah Muied & Marra Sherrier

First Edition: January 2025

Recommended Grade Level: Grade 2–3

Dedication

This book series is dedicated to all past and present stakeholders in NY Unlocking Futures: staff, volunteers, board members and financial contributors.

Acknowledgements & Appreciation

Thank you to all of our young people, mentors, youth-service professionals, educators, & parents who have used the "Curriculum of Possibilities" to transform the quality of their lives.

We would also like to thank the Karl Richard Lane Educational Fund for their generous support in making this project possible.

Unlocking Futures:
Empowering Growth & Transformation

Who We Are:

Unlocking Futures is a nonprofit organization committed to transforming the lives of young people by breaking barriers and building brighter futures. For over 40 years, our Curriculum for Possibilities has empowered youth to develop self-confidence, achieve success in education and relationships, and unlock their full potential.

Our impact spans 26 states and six continents, reaching diverse groups including foster youth, participants in juvenile justice programs, and students in world-renowned institutions. From Brown University in the United States to Ashoka University in India, Unlocking Futures demonstrates the universal power of its transformational approach.

Whether you're a parent, teacher, mentor, or simply someone curious about self-growth, this book serves as a powerful tool for inner child work and collective growth- designed to help kids and adults thrive together.

Our Evolution:

Initially focused on youth development, Unlocking Futures expanded over the decades to include the adults who influence young people—parents, mentors, teachers, and counselors. We discovered that when these adults adopt and embody the Curriculum for Possibilities, their impact on youth grows exponentially.

By scaling our program to include those who guide and mentor, we created a ripple effect: one parent can influence several children, one teacher can inspire an entire classroom, and one counselor can shape generations of students.

As adults integrate the curriculum into their own lives, they not only teach its principles but also live them, creating a foundation for lasting, positive change.

How to Use This Book

As part of the Unlocking Futures Curriculum Book Series, Trust Takes a Chance is designed to be more than just a story—it's a teaching tool for growth and transformation. Whether you're a parent, teacher, mentor, or counselor, this book helps both adults and young people navigate self-growth together.

For Adults First: Before sharing this book with a young person, read it yourself and complete the review questions. This step allows you to reflect on the lessons personally, making it easier to guide meaningful conversations. Then, use the lesson plans to facilitate discussion and engagement.

Without this preparation, the book remains just a story. But with your guidance, it becomes a powerful tool for learning, connection, and change.

Meet **Trust**

1

Meet **Jojo**, Trust's Best Friend

Meet **Maine**, Salesperson at *Just Try It* Sneaker Store

Trust is faced with a difficult situation. He calls his best friend Jojo to help him work it out.

Trust says. "Hi, Jojo!"

"Hey, Trust! What are you doing right now?" Jojo responds.

Trust answers, "I'm walking to this sneaker store called *Just Try It*. I need to change my game."

Jojo is curious now. She asks, "Oh, what game are you trying to change?"

Trust replies, "Well, I want a special girl to notice me tonight at the party. You know who she is."

Jojo adds, “Haha! So, you want Destiny to notice and dance with you, huh?”

“Yes! I want her to talk to me too and think I’m the coolest guy ever!” Trust replies.

“What exactly are you going to look for at the sneaker store?” she asks.

“You know me!” says Trust.

Jojo responds, “Yeah, yeah. I know!”

Jojo adds, “And I bet you’re planning to spend no more than $50 on your black sneakers too.”

Then she continues to ask, “Why do you like them so much? Don’t you see you’re just repeating the past?”

Trust ponders, “Um, I never thought too deeply about it. I can’t change my mind. I like what I like, and I like black sneakers, that's all! I have always worn black sneakers- ever since I was a little kid.”

Trust's Closet

Jojo gently responds, "Yeah, Trust, but you're not a little kid anymore. It's time to STOP living in the past."

"Hmm. Could you meet me at the store?" he asks timidly.

"Sounds good. I've been to *Just Try It*. I know exactly where it is. I'll meet you there in a few."

At the store:
"Welcome to *Just Try It.* My name is Maine—I'm your sneaker expert for today. How can I help you?"

Maine asks, "Are you looking for something special? We just got some cool new arrivals!"

Before Maine could finish, Trust runs to find the familiar black sneakers.

Maine exclaims, "Wow! I see you already knew what you were coming in for today!"

As Jojo arrives, she sees Trust reaching for the black sneakers and says,

“Oh, Trust. Not another pair of black sneakers..”

Jojo continues: “Trust, I know that you think you are shopping, but you’re not really shopping at all! Your past and old habits are shopping!"

Jojo continues: “You’re supposed to be shopping for something new, but you are picking something similar to what you already own.”

“You know Destiny’s going to be at the party, and you haven’t been able to get her attention yet."

“If you want different results, you’ve gotta do things differently! Trust, shop for the future and let go of past habits!”

Maine then adds, “Years ago, black sneakers were in, but not now colors are what's in style now! You can see it everywhere on social media!”

Trust shouts, “No way! I just can’t! No! No! No!”

Jojo refocuses Trust,

“Okay, okay. Let’s do a reset. What are you wearing tonight?” Trust says, “I’m thinking about wearing a white tee, these purple pants, and my black sneakers, of course.”

Jojo replies, “That’s cool. I like it. What would make a difference is if you went with these yellow and white sneakers! Switching it up could get Destiny’s attention. Especially since she has never noticed you in the black ones before.”

Trust hesitates, “Color? I’m really uncomfortable with that. I’ve never worn sneakers with color before. I don’t even want to try it on. And they cost $85. That’s just too much!”

Jojo replies: “Just ***TRY IT ON***. Trying new things and changing old habits will be uncomfortable. But, Trust, think about what you want to have happen tonight. You may have to be uncomfortable if you really want Destiny’s attention.”

“I don’t know...” says Trust.

Jojo stresses, “These new colorful sneakers really could change what happens tonight, Trust. Would you just try them on?”

Still unsure, he says, “I’m really uncomfortable.”

Jojo reminds Trust, “This is your choice. I know you are uncomfortable, but we cannot make you try them on. It’s up to you to choose."

Jojo continues, “Remember what I told you! Breaking habits can be uncomfortable, but… breaking old habits creates new possibilities. And after a while, Trust, you will become comfortable being uncomfortable.”

Maine adds, “Then you will take more chances, try new things, and grow!”

Trust thinks about this for a moment then replies, “Okay, okay! I’ll try them on, but I’m not happy!”

Trust sits on the couch at the store and puts on the colorful sneakers. He is surprised by how cool he looks! He begins to feel different.

Trust can't contain his smile and shouts, "They look better than I could have imagined!"

"They are HOT! You know, I *will* buy these sneakers!"

Jojo says ecstatically, "I'm so happy for you, Trust, for trying something new even though you were uncomfortable. Your surprised expression of joy has made my day! You've created a new future when you let go of your past. I just know Destiny will notice you tonight!"

At the party, Trust has a great time dancing with his new colorful kicks! He even gets to talk and dance with Destiny!

The next day, he calls Jojo and replays the night.

Trust reflects,

"Thanks to you and Maine, now I know that *trying on new things* can make me feel uncomfortable at first, but it doesn't have to stay that way. "

Trust continues, “You know, I used to only think about the past, and I didn’t do anything different to change my path.

I never imagined *trying on something new* would create such a different experience for me.

Making new choices feels powerful!”

Let's Review!

REFLECTION

Remember, like Jojo helped Trust at the sneaker store, you might have people in your life who believe in your potential and want to see you grow. Their advice or encouragement might feel uncomfortable at first—because it's new!

But here's the exciting part: trying something new can lead to new possibilities. Just like Trust learned, to have something you've never had before, you have to be brave enough to step out of your comfort zone.

Think about it: what could be waiting for you on the other side of that uncomfortable feeling?

A new opportunity, a new friend, or even a new version of YOU!

Let's dive into some questions to help you find your own "Try-On" moment.

Remember: You are not just 'trying to' do something, you are "Trying-it-On!" Put those sneakers on!

[*Get a Pencil, Paper (or Keyboard!) ready and continue to the next Page*]

(Parents and guardians, consider these question in your own life, past and present. Choose examples you could share. Optionally, consider a challenge you might "Try-on" for yourself in partnership with your young person.)

Let's Review!

TRY-ON CHALLENGE: QUESTIONS TO HELP YOU GROW

Find your "sneaker store" moment:

1. Think about a part of your life where you want to see a big change or feel more confident.

Is it at school? With friends? At home? Trying a new activity?

What is one thing you'd love to do better or differently?

Find your "black sneakers":

2. Are there things you keep doing the same way that might be limiting your potential? Write it down.

(For example, always sitting alone at lunch, sticking to one subject you're good at, or avoiding new things because they feel scary.)

Ask (and answer) yourself:

3. Are you willing to feel a little uncomfortable to have a new outcome?

(Sometimes it feels weird or hard at first, but it's how we grow!)

Let's Review!

TRY-ON CHALLENGE: QUESTIONS TO HELP YOU GROW

Imagine your "colorful shoes":

4. What's one new thing you could "try-on" to get a different result?

(Need help? Ask a friend, parent, or teacher for ideas—they're like Jojo, here to support you!)

Step into action:

5. Take a brave step! Choose one thing to try-on in your "sneaker store moment." Write it down or tell your Jojo about it.

After you've tried it, think:

- *How did it feel?*
- *What did you learn?*
- *Do you want to try more new things in the future?*

Celebrate your "new shoes" moment

6. Think of a time you tried something different and it worked out better than you expected.

What happened? How did it feel? Would you do it again?

Let's Review!

TRY-ON CHALLENGE: QUESTIONS TO HELP YOU GROW

Who's your support squad?

7. Who could cheer you on, encourage you, or remind you of your strength when trying something new?

Write down one person you trust or admire that you could turn to.

Spot your "comfort zone habit"

8. What's something you keep doing because it's easy, familiar, or safe — but might be holding you back?

Write down one habit, decision, or situation you always stick to. (Example: Only hanging out with the same people, saying no to new things, or telling yourself "I can't.")

Not sure where to start? Here are some examples to help you think about your own "Try-On" moments:

Let's Review!

EXAMPLES

HEALTH

Maybe you want to get stronger or faster so you can do better in gym class or join a sports team. But instead of playing outside, you're in the habit of sitting on the couch.

→ "Try-on" going for a run or playing catch with a friend

You want to eat more fruits and veggies, but you always choose chips.

→ "Try-on" tasting a new kind of fruit, like kiwi or mango

FRIENDS & FAMILY

Is there someone you want to be closer to, like a sibling, friend, parent or someone you've lost contact with?

→ "Try-on" sending them a message or inviting them to do something fun together

Do you want to make new friends, but you've been sitting alone at lunch?

→ "Try-on" saying "hi" to someone new or joining a game at recess

EDUCATION

Have you been dreaming about learning a new skill, like playing the piano, drawing, or coding? But instead, you keep spending your free time watching TV or playing video games?

→ "Try-on" setting aside 15 minutes a day to practice

Is there a subject at school, like math or reading, that you want to get better at?

→ "Try-on" asking a teacher, tutor, or parent for support or use a fun learning app!

HOBBIES & FUN

Are you bored and seeking new ways to express yourself?

→ "Try-on" something new, like painting, baking or designing a new game!

About the Authors

The Faisons are sought after coaches, facilitators, and retreat leaders. Their work with Unlocking Futures, formerly known as Youth At Risk, impacts the lives of thousands of youth, working in 26 States and 6 continents

The Faison's use their platform to uplift.

For booking contact info@nyunlockingfutures.org

Testimonials

"The young people who are now thriving, contributing adults are living testimonials to the transformative work of Unlocking Futures. When I first encountered this organization in 1992, I saw firsthand how its unique methodology helped youth break free from hardened narratives of despair and impossibility. Unlike traditional child welfare approaches, Unlocking Futures equips young people with the tools and social capital to rewrite their stories and create bright, hopeful futures. This work is truly life-changing."

Willie Tolliver, Professor, The Silberman School of Social Work at Hunter College

"With its Curriculum for Possibilities, Unlocking Futures has transformed young lives for over 25 years, breaking cycles of incarceration and offering a brighter future for youth. At a fraction of the $140,000 yearly cost of residential facilities, their proven approach saves millions while creating real, lasting change."

Luther Garrison, Juvenile Probation Officer for 22 years

"I became involved with Unlocking Futures in 1997, seeking an opportunity to work directly with young people and make a meaningful difference beyond my legal pro bono work. Over the years, I've served as a mentor, Board Chairperson, and advisor, witnessing firsthand the life-changing impact of this organization. Unlocking Futures' programs provide critical support, improving self-esteem, academic achievement, and overall well-being for young people, often in life-saving ways. I've seen participants overcome challenges, graduate, and lead fulfilling, productive lives—proof of the organization's profound and lasting impact."

Hon. Sherri Eisenpress, Family Court Judge

www.ingramcontent.com/pod-product-compliance
Ingram Content Group UK Ltd.
Pitfield, Milton Keynes, MK11 3LW, UK
UKRC040054200726
13851UKWH00024B/67